Jen's Best Gift Ever

Written by
Laura Appleton-Smith

Illustrated by
Keinyo White

A Book to Remember™
Published by Flyleaf Publishing
Post Office Box 185, Lyme, NH 03768

For orders or information, contact us at **(800) 449-7006**.
Please visit our website at **www.flyleafpublishing.com**

First Edition
Library of Congress Catalog Card Number: 98-96630
ISBN 0-9658246-2-4

To LAS for her unwavering faith and patience,
and for my wife.

KW

For Bailey.

LAS

It is six o'clock and the sun is just up.

Jen lifts back her quilt and jumps from bed.

She runs to the calendar next to her desk.
At last, it is Jen's birthday!

"I am seven–seven, seven, seven," she sings
as she runs to tell Mom and Dad.

Just as Jen gets to Mom and Dad's bed she stops…

On the rug next to the bed is a gift box.
It has a big ribbon on the top.

"Happy Birthday Jen," sing Mom and Dad, and Jen's sister Emma.

They tell Jen to lift the lid from the box.

She lifts the lid…

In the box, snug in a soft blanket, is a black kitten.

Jen lifts the kitten up.

"What will I name him?" she asks.

Just then the kitten jumps from Jen's hands.

He lands on the rug and runs under Mom and Dad's bed.

The kitten is hidden under the bed and Jen cannot get him out.

Jen has a plan.

She pulls a strand of ribbon from the gift box.

Jen drags the ribbon on the rug next to the bed.

The kitten runs out and snags the ribbon.
He jumps and twists and flips as he runs after it.

"I will name him Frolic," Jen tells Emma.

"Frolic is the best name for a kitten that can run and jump so well."

Frolic runs and jumps and flips and spins
until he has to rest. Jen lifts him onto her lap.

She thanks Mom and Dad.

A kitten is the best gift Jen has ever had.